Thursday Night Special

Chandra Steele

For my mother, who taught me beginning, middle,
and end

Contents

Take a Number

The most salient fact she has so far about death is that it has at least as much bureaucracy as life. She's still waiting for processing. She's pretty sure it's day three.

The plastic seats are chipped. They're the same cheap mass-produced mid-century replicas you'd find in an outdated DMV. She strums a shard of semi-separated laminate, the vibration resonating dully around her, duplicating the thick repetitive feeling in the center of her brain.

She loops back to what she remembers since the after. It starts with the bus. She doesn't recall its outside. There's just the memory of being in what gave the appearance of a mostly empty airport shuttle. It must have taken her to this center but disembarking is yet another gap in events. There was a queue of sorts once she got here. And there's been the waiting ever since. That's all she has.

No one she's come in contact with has given her any information unless it's been related directly to the business at hand. It's possible she hasn't asked any-one. She has trouble interrogating even her own thoughts. Communication feels beyond the bounds of her abilities and desires, beyond necessity.

She knows that they are signing her up for all new cards and things with the ten-digit number she's been assigned. It's not the same as her social security one and she's had persistent worry about keeping it straight. The concern enters her head from one side and leaves from the other, and when it returns, she has only the vaguest sense that it's traveled that path in her brain before.

Her mother is talking to the clerk, giving them some of the information she herself was not able to convey. She's spent nearly two years missing her mother but she doesn't believe she's told her that or even looked directly at her. She became aware of her presence after what was likely several minutes of her mother standing over her, the repeated request for her personal details finally becoming intelligible to her. She'd silently slipped out the same smooth black wallet she'd had for years and handed it over. She was mildly surprised that some of her belongings like her wallet and bag were with her and seemed necessary.

On the way here, she'd passed a salon. It jutted out as a little obsidian square at the end of the curving cul-de-sac of a town that resembled the place she'd lived until she was eight. The stores were set up a little differently, the way it is in dreams, and now as it seems in death. The windows seamlessly cut around the corner of the salon and inside was the warmth of people with activity and purpose. The lights inside were peacefully reassuring against the darkening evening sky outside and she felt like she could remain there forever.

Maybe it was something she'd constructed in her mind or maybe it had been made up for her to feel more comfortable with this new situation. It was the sort of scene that before would have made her ache for a normal day out with her mother and she drifted calmly on the feeling that maybe they could have that here.

Since her mother died, she'd dreamt nightly of her. Pretty much the same thing, with variations. You're going to die, she'd tell her. Did you know? In a month. Three months. A year. You already died. Why are you walking around? How do you feel? Her mother's eyes never fully registered what she was saying or that she was there. The last dream she'd had like that was still with her.

She had been sitting in the Volvo station wagon that was the last car her mother owned, but in the backseat, where she would have sat decades before. Her mother was at the wheel and they were passing a ramshackle building. She remarked that it had once been a place where they would have lunch together. Her mother had no comment. She leaned forward over the armrest in the front row and repeated herself. No answer from her mother. She got louder still and her mother turned slowly, eyes unregistering, no words forthcoming. She asked her mother to please recall it, please tell her how she was going to go on without her.

Here her mother has the extreme competence she had in life, talking to the person behind the Lexan about her with authority. She sees her wallet in her hand and she has another thought from life, of approaching front desks and doctors and nurses and reciting numbers, her mother's birth date, her social security number, the dates of her diagnosis and admissions, her average oxygen saturation levels. Each time she did it she felt increasingly feverish, the paperwork she had to fill out blurred a little more, until she couldn't even make out the foot-tall indications of what floor she was on in the hospital.

It's one of the clearest thoughts she's had here but she pushes it out of her mind and feels the daze settle back. She stares at the new card in her hand, repeats the numbers over and over and wonders what will be attached to this new numerical identity.

Boy, You Turn Me

Like a switch flipped in his brain. A metaphor. But this was real. At least the sound was.

The click was loud, leaned mechanical. A large industrial on/off that could only be moved with great effort and even greater authority. The thunk reverberated with its own irreversibility.

And just like that his world turned upside down. The line connecting his brain and his ocular nerves shut down production for unstated reasons, right in the middle of an intersection.

He sunk to his knees and crawled to the corner. His head bent low to the curb, the street across straight up as his hair scraped the pavement.

Someone called an ambulance. There were so many people yelling things at him at each other at people they were on the phone with. Upside-down people he was meeting for the first time. Afterward even people he knew his whole life were new to him, with their feet in the air, dangling from the sky every time he looked at them.

A new perspective. That is what the therapist said he had. In his life now where nothing was what it seemed to be, everything was a lot more straightforward.

The illusions that his brain was manufacturing, he saw through them all the second it cut out talking to his eyes about everything.

Colors were meaningless. Before someone could tell him the ocean was blue and he would say yes it's blue but whose blue because who could tell if his blue was their blue and so now it was no color. And the streets and birds and planes were no color because they all could be any color.

Time moved backward in front of him and forward behind him and sometimes the other way around or not at all if he got super close up to something.

He wondered if entire galaxies could experience such shifts, collapsing in on themselves and then popping back inside out.

That noise he heard, maybe it wasn't a big bang lowercase but a Big Bang uppercase. The stars seen at night, so many of them are dead, so long ago but if he could go all the way out there and stand on one of them and look back home through his legs, by the time he folded himself over, the planet would be snuffed out, gone, nothing to see here.

Not My Baby

I was into rom-coms for too long. The biggest risk I've taken is I went to Nepal to do relief work, fell in love with a German woman, brought her back to Brooklyn. It could not have turned out worse. I recently discovered that the closer a wound is to your heart, the faster the healing time.

The first round is on me if you can hang in a serious dive bar.

Together we could find a new form of life or just talk physics. We could go upstate for apple pie. What English word do you think sounds best? A random fact I love is zebras are black animals with white stripes. Two truths and a lie: when I get nervous my left eyebrow shakes, I walked Manhattan end to end in less than two hours, I once accidentally auditioned for porn.

What if I told you that I frequently get paid to travel to allegedly haunted places.

I was briefly held hostage in Laos while mildly tripping on mushrooms.

I saved a dog from getting run over by a car in Ireland.

I had to evade a drug smuggler in Morocco.

I was detained in Singapore and Cuba.

I'm Marc, Greg, Shawn, Leo, Louis-Francois, Aaron, Becket. The secret to getting to know me is: don't discuss politics with me.

My go-to karaoke song is "Take Me Home, Country Roads." My fondest childhood memory is beekeeping with the old man. I won't shut up about, I dunno, books and shit. Believe it or not, I have Bill Murray's phone number.

Like you I live in Crown Heights, Bushwick, New Jersey, Philly, currently am abroad but might move back to the States. Believe it or not, I am leaving New York in the summer so it's probably best not to fall in love unless you want to quit your job and travel the world with me.

I'm a copywriter, software engineer, creative director, design mercenary. I'm a professor at college. That guy who answers all of your tech questions. I have a job. A life goal of mine is to be the first Mars archaeologist. Believe it or not, I don't use any social media. I am, for real, a bird watcher.

What do I think about organized religion? You could say I'm agnostic. I'm an atheist. Agnostic and an atheist. I'm spiritual. Believe it or not, I used to be a Mormon. Please don't be into astrology.

It's really surprising that I don't like beets, iced tea, or rice krispies treats. My simple pleasures are sunsets mostly. If loving smooth jazz is wrong, I don't want to be right. I'd donate a kidney for tickets to "Springsteen on Broadway" but now it's on Netflix. This year I really want to actually learn to speak French. Give me travel tips for tropical islands where I can learn to surf and scuba dive and not think about politics anymore.

I'm looking for someone with a warm smile who is active and has a bit of an edge. An emotionally and mentally healthy, attractive, intelligent woman. All I ask is that you be cool, be yourself, have confidence, don't get uncomfortable too easily, and want to laugh at silly things. The most influential woman in my life is my grandmother who once told me I look like "the establishment on vacation." Who says Grandma can't help me get laid. My most irrational fear is sinkholes.

Guess where this photo was taken. Here's a picture of me with sharp implements, oysters, heart-shaped mylar balloons, a Mustang that's not mine, a cat that's not mine, a baby that's not mine, a girl with the mind-blown emoji over her head who is no longer mine. I don't know that guy back there. This is a bathroom selfie but I liked the light.

I have been known to smile, I swear. I'm weirdly attracted to texting in complete, grammatically correct sentences. You should not go out with me if you deify anyone. I want someone who can call me out on my BS. I'm looking for someone who is interested in a slow burn. I'm a busy boy. I've sequestered one weekend day for dates. We'll get along if you don't take yourself all too seriously and can laugh at yourself and, of course, others. I'm looking for a reason to leave work early. I want someone who brings some happiness into my life. All I ask is that you be kind.

Sic Transit Memoria

Here's what we would have talked about today if we were still talking.

New York City buses. On my lunchtime walk I remembered how much I used to love riding the bus on beautiful spring days. Something about the way it lumbers along like a drowsy, heavy bee in the sweet air. There's a forced intimacy that's the opposite of that impenetrable zone you form around you on the subway. People say "hi," thank the driver, show each other what they bought at Fairway.

I've also been thinking about Norwegian serial killers. I was reading about that case and how pleasant and humane the prisons are in Norway. There's no death penalty and jail terms are short but there's hardly any repeat crime.

Remember how we saw that movie "Tokyo!" and that demon thing that blew the city to carnage just disappeared at his own execution? That's all we really want with executions, for the thing that committed them to just go away. In Norway they know that but here we mistake it for bloodlust.

After that movie we went to a bar. We talked about the tattoo buttons on the pizza delivery girl's arm:

Fear, Love, Time. The shut-in pressed Love and the
streets shook. You thought that meant it was the end. I
said it was the beginning.

Without anything as straightforward as a button, I
hailed a cab. You'd wanted more. We didn't speak for
a while. I thought it was the end. It was the beginning.

Lives of the Saints

Sebastian

Sebastian woke with a strong urge to make some toast. His toaster required vigilance. The coils in the middle were dead so he counted out ninety seconds, hit cancel, flipped the slices, counted again.

The kitchen floor tiles were solid with November cold so he put down the loaf of bread and went to get some socks from the drawer next to the window in his bedroom. This violated his arrangement of completing all his morning tasks in a counterclockwise order and he hoped nothing bad would happen to him later as a result.

Once he'd forgotten his walking cap after he'd already crossed the hall to the coat closet and gone into the kitchen to check that all the knobs on the stove were in a strict twelve to six alignment. Instead of going right out the door as he should have, he walked across to the hat rack, took his cap off it, placed it on his head, and then crossed the parquet diagonally. Hours later he was hit by a cab.

For now the socks were reassuringly warm and he was unafraid of the risk. He went back to his Wonder Bread.

Renee stood before the throngs emerging from underground. The missives she held in her hand were damp from her clutching them and the ink had gone runny. But she felt sure her messages would still get through.

She composed them in even capital letters. The same thing written on each sheet each day but not the same thing every day. She took her cues from three local newspapers, cracking the code that she knew lay in each and assembling the words so that their meaning was plain.

They'd stopped selling the notebooks she had been writing them in for years but she'd found a decent substitute. The blue felt-tip pens she favored had been on store shelves her whole life.

She wrote her letters every day from noon to six. It worked out well because it let her reach commuters in the morning, when they weren't all awake enough to refuse her and one or two would end up with a crumpled sheet in their hands and she still had time to visit her favorite place to pick up produce and fix dinner.

Maybe today they'd have some good brussels sprouts, she thought, as she brushed her lightly stained hands against her soft coat.

He removed two low branches from the tree. They were pliable with early spring life running through them. He affixed the branches to his head. He didn't even want to talk about god today, he decided.

He felt like a Roman. Or was it the Greeks who wore them?

Nature was always his thing, even when he was young. Some neighbor kids back when he was eight had gotten an Atari and charged a nickel for three games of Duck Hunt. There was a line out their living room but you could always find him outside instead.

He imagined the narrow alleyway next to his house was a bit of bayou. The scraggly sticks making their way through the cracked concrete, a patch of cypress, the bugs that scuttled past, rare breeds of frog. The closest body of water was miles away but if he tried hard enough on humid days, he could smell the radiating warmth of swamp and mud.

That's where he needed to be now, near some water. He straightened his branches and headed to the B train to go to 72nd St.

He would cross the street when they moved on. They'd been following him since 14th St. and he hoped he could lose them at the crosswalk. It was too hard to hear what they were saying but he thought he caught his name when he stopped and pretended to examine a discarded bottle and they got close.

He'd shaken their cohorts earlier. He could tell they were together because they all had the same coat. Black with two rows of shiny black buttons. Innocuous-looking discs to those who didn't notice things so well as he but all exactly the same size with a raised rim, four holes, stitches sewn in a criss-cross.

His eyes were a clear blue. That was part of how he had such keen sight. Instead of information sinking into a dark void, his captured everything and held it on their bright surface, like mirrored trays.

His grandfather had those eyes, his mother told him. He'd taken off and left her and her mother when she was three but she remembered his eyes and nothing else, not even the shape of him as he walked out the door after he'd kissed the top of her head.

Eyes like that didn't let anything out, which was the only fortunate thing he could see about his present circumstance. People could track him and jostle him and map his comings and goings but they'd never get inside because they couldn't see into those shining eyes.

He turned them to the grey unbroken sky and they cut it cleaner than a skyscraper.

The Copy Artist

They told him he had the hands of an archivist which he thought was a poetic thing to say until he found out the person who had the job before him had torn most of the letters. He didn't know if there were any other requirements for the job or if he met them but they hired him and so now he had a thing to say when he was at parties.

There was drama in the work and that he liked. His space was behind a mahogany panel in the gift shop. He'd step through, put down his bag and coat, remove anything extraneous like a watch that could catch against an envelope or a belt that could brush against a stray paper when he stood up, and then he'd put on a fresh pair of white gloves and push aside a deep red velvet curtain to get to the shelves. It was quiet in there and cool. The only heat came from him and the thin aluminum laptop on which he typed.

He removed a letter, the next one in the stack, and transcribed. In the time between the 32nd letter in box 3a and the 33rd one he'd just removed from the same box, he'd dreamt of his dog. She had walked into a room with a Persian carpet and lain down, resurrected but so thin that her skin was shiny where it wrapped around her ribs. She hadn't been like that in life. He soothed her and pet her and thanked her for coming because he knew that it must have taken great effort for her to visit him from the dead.

So far his father hadn't made the trip. It was something he thought about while reading the words of the handwritten letters and turning them into Times New Roman. His father's last words had been the same as all his others: deliberately inconsequential, impersonal, sans serif.

It was a shame, really, what he did. The letters lost so much in the transition. The paper chosen, the color of ink, the slant or straightness of 26 symbols of speech and he flattened their meaning. He would read them on the screen after he was done and it was like a bad overdub of a show that stripped out the tone.

His dog got up after their visit and left with the politeness and dignity she had conveyed in her 15 years. He knew her in his bones and so she was able to live there in his mind. He remembered his father for who he was to him but not for who he was. Maybe that was why he was reluctant to show up, to make a journey that far only to be misinterpreted when he got there.

The therapist said he should express his grief in a letter. But his own feelings were unknown to him. Sometimes a sentence from one of the boxes sounded right and he thought about borrowing it but it wasn't his and so he put it back away.

Bill of Goods

Watch your step. That door saddle always gets me. I lost a cute chunky heel to it last week.

The wall hanging is from Ulan Bator. We went there on our third date. On our first date we were talking about that couple that on their first date backpacked through Europe together for a month. So we thought if we made it to a third date we'd spend three months doing that through Asia. On our second date we did those questions that make you fall in love so we made it to our second date OK. There's not a price on the wall hanging but like...$500? I could let it go for $500.

What about living-room things? This ottoman is amazing. Johan and I eat dinner on it. We don't really cook because we like to keep all the kitchen things clean for when people come through. But we arrange takeout on the little tray on that buffet over there and then put it on top of the ottoman and it's perfect. The tray isn't for sale yet. It's part of a collaboration we're doing but I don't think I can talk about it yet. The ottoman is $3,000.

Collaborations are weird. We sat down with them. I really can't tell you who they are but I promise you, you have been to one of their stores. Like just a couple stops away they have a location. To think of walking in and seeing something with our names on it in that beautiful setting near the bridge in Dumbo. Just ugh. I cannot wait.

But working with them was a lot. We told them all our ideas and they listened and were polite and all but then they were like, "Here's how we can refine what you've come up with for our like 100 stores here." And we had sketched out all these things. Not on paper, but with our words, and then they came back with these trays and a throw blanket. They're great though and our name will be on them like I said.

Our business is probably going to go through the roof when it does. Hahaha I didn't even mean it that way. Though I am kind of trying to keep it on the DL from the landlord. I don't think he reads the sites or anything. The *Times* called and they might come by and profile us because how many people are there living their complete lives but also constantly selling it, too? It's a compelling story. Sometimes I stop and think about it and it even moves me and I'm the one doing it. Well me and Johan. We have bathroom stuff, too, if you want to go in there. Cute fluffy mats and towels. Let's go look at the toothbrush cup. It's this marble that you can only get from one quarry in the Italian Alps.

Here's a weird thing that happened. When we were setting this up I wondered if it violated the lease or anything to be selling stuff out of here. I mean we really do live here and use everything, that's the point. But I didn't know if having people walk through and making it all buyable was totally legal. All those Airbnb stories, you know? They're still around and everything though so. What was I saying?

Oh yeah so I wanted to look at the lease. It's really Johan's place and I just moved in after we got back from Asia. So I went over to his desk in the bedroom. Oh, let me show it to you. It's from this guy in Iowa. He was making them in a lot a few blocks away for a while out of just stuff he found on the street. Anyway I went in there to find the lease and when I was reading it I noticed that it said "John" on it and not "Johan." Isn't that strange?

I asked him about it when he got home. "Is your name Johan or is it John?" He said, "My parents named me John but I feel like Johan." I mean I can totally respect that but I felt a little funny for a while. I get it: do you, be who you want to be, don't let anyone define you especially your parents, right? But I fell in love with Johan on that second date. I traveled with Johan. Who is John? Does he live here?

See anything you want?

Pushed

You check for the train. You lean slightly over the edge but only just a bit. Enough to brace yourself. Because it's not only being pushed, you figure.

There are the elderly women, blank-eyed to anything around them, three bags deep on either side—at least two of them capacious and plaid and plastic—fanned out like low-lying wings that could buffet you off the platform. There are the private dancers and singers, old-school headphones cupped over their ears, one shut-eyed moonwalk from plunging you to possible electrocution or death by locomotive. There are the gaggles of girls who in another time or place would be women but are now spike-heeled and the subject of all their own sentences, teetering dangerously on the hobnailed yellow strip, likely to take you down with them.

Don't push me!" you hear. You look past the stanchion you were prepared to grasp. An average girl with average hair and average clothes and average looks has distinguished herself. Arms flailing, phone in hand, body facing the train-less tunnel but her eyes and the tilt of her head accusing the woman behind her.

Why would this woman push anyone? She's on the wrong end of suburbia and her 40s, elasticized jeans already in place. Her turtleneck has the same pattern of tightly spaced rosettes found on the underwear of five-year-old girls—neither should be seen in public.

"I said: Don't push me!" And now you hate that you just witnessed this woman and her ashy blonde hair clearly not push this girl. Because if it's not the shifting weight of her backpack combined with a resident paranoia, this girl could be looking for a cover story. A reason to throw herself in front of the train that just won't arrive. Thirteen minutes already, seriously. And then you'd have to decide if you'd stick around to talk to the police or if you'd get on the train they'd send to the track behind you to take away the now-distressed platform of people from the suicide/murder scene, your choice. They'd have to send another train, right?

But the girl is alive for now and she's yelling into her phone at a sustained volume and pitch that reminds you of a minaret and you're ready to face east and fall to your knees right there in the suffocating underground and pray to Allah for her to stop. "This motherfucker tried to push me! I will not calm down! Why are you judging me?" she yells into her phone.

Now the woman gets some chutzpah. "Why would I push her?" she says loudly to the man next to her. "I don't even know this bitch." You reassess. She's not a tourist, she's from New Jersey.

"You hate me!" the girl wails and it's not immediately clear who she's addressing but you're sure she's right.

She must have meant the person on the phone because she now puts it in her pocket and whirls to face the woman. "Stop touching me!" she yells across the three-foot distance between them. You hear a rumble and instead of throwing herself in front of the train or preparing to board it, she stomps off toward the stairs. "I have bedbugs! And I hope you have them now, too!" The train's approaching. You look at everyone around you. And you want to push them over the edge, every last one.

Out of the Blue

I looked into your milky blue depths. Your whole inner self up there on that glowing screen while the doctors rushed around. The two segments of your brain each have their own lumpy outline. They don't look like you. They have none of your smoothness, your parabolic curves.

The only thing that reminds me of you is the tulip shape of your fallopian tubes, the budding of your ovaries. How strange that you carry all your potential children around with you. If I knew what I was looking at, I could tell you when to start to worry, when to ask me about where things are going, where's my head at, do I see a future.

My potential children have a turnover rate nearly equal to the versions of you that have passed through my life. If they leave, more will take their place. Sometimes I wonder if my sperm know this when they follow their urge to swim upstream and are instead trapped like factory-farmed salmon.

You can't teach a four-year-old about evolution and reproduction in the same breath but my mother did and the two concepts became bound together. All life grew out of the sea but I grew out of you, I used to think when I looked at her. How could that be? Time, to a child, whether it's five minutes or five thousand years, all has the same fuzzy bendability.

Maybe when I emerged I was a horseshoe crab. Maybe you were an elaborately reticulated seahorse.

Thursday Night Special

"If I was writing this story I would start at the red door," he said from the top of the steps.

She wrapped her arms around her and rubbed her hands against her thin sweater. It was a May night; average warmth for New York, no precipitation. The sweater, filmy black sleeveless dress, and ballet flats that made up her outfit were meant to go from work to work-related happy hour. If it had been too cold or too rainy or too anything she could use it as an excuse not to be on the sidewalk for another minute and turn and walk home. But not so much as a breeze swung the carved-wood sign that hung from a pole above the door. Le Lumiere it said in fancy lettering but shed no light on what went on inside.

Even though he was about to press the buzzer, he'd had his own reservations earlier. "Let's just see who goes in," he'd said when they'd approached the building. They made a pass but on the entire block there were just two women, one concerned with hailing a cab and the other with curbing her wiry dog. They kept walking until both were gone and then retraced their own steps.

"In 30 minutes we could each be at home watching Netflix." He looked at her to gauge her reaction. "Or we could be in there."

The flat red of the door gave off a sudden intensity and they moved slightly closer. They locked eyes in a nonverbal dare. He broke. "Let's do it," he said and strode up the three shallow concrete steps. She was behind until she noticed a very tiny window that had been covered up by a sliding metal gate whenever she'd passed by during the day. It was sort of charming in its diminutive size, even with the tacky sheer purple curtains parted around a small shaded lamp. A small red lamp.

"There's an actual red light," she yelled up to him but he was oblivious now that he had done the thing that would get them inside, so she joined him. Their anticipation was all that filled the silence. Then suddenly, a high-pitched whirring started up.

"I think I hear vacuuming," she said. "Do you hear vacuuming?"

"At least it's clean."

"Well that's what you want in a sex club," she said. A buzz and a click and a turn of a knob later and her skills of audio identification should never have been in doubt because before them an older man was stooped over an upright vacuum that was as much of a relic as he was. He moved the cord so they could sidestep him up two stairs whose carpeting had received too much of his attention over who knows how many years.

It was hard to tell if the foyer's swank was past its prime or just poorly executed. There was a booth with a black faux-marble counter and some red velvet curtains held back by braided mustard-colored ropes. A small gold bell to ring for service sat there but wasn't needed, though the booth's occupant barely moved her eyes from her phone. "Welcome," she said. "Tonight it is a hundred and fifteen dollars."

"Oh, the Thursday night price," he said, his voice trying to sound knowing but cracking as he placed fresh, uncreased bills on the counter.

They'd stopped at a Chase on the way over. "I'll pay," he'd said earlier outside the bar, with an air of graciousness, like it was the accepted and gentlemanly thing to do when you suggest to an acquaintance that you visit a sex club together.

There'd always been something unexplored between them and when everyone else had parted ways outside the bar they'd hung back. He was charming and sharp and funny and that was as big a warning to her as a rotted lung and 24-point type on a pack of cigarettes. They'd unwind from conversations with others and drift together at all such get-togethers. Not that she was smooth in every social situation, but she'd trip over her thoughts when she talked to him, echoes of a thing she said reverberating as the alcohol she consumed retreated from her brain later.

His jokes would often touch on his being Muslim, and they caused an ache of the familiar in her chest that increased her attraction to him. They were no different than the shtick her relatives used as a shield when they were ghettoized and targeted for genocide. Her own humor could never stick a landing with finesse in response, ungainly as it was from the sympathy it came loaded with. She unfortunately had a very sharp recollection of the time she told him very sincerely that she hoped one day the tenor in the country would change so that he could enjoy the sort of turnaround Woody Allen had, going from being banned from the New York Athletic Club to enjoying the aegis of white privilege. "May you one day live happily married to your stepdaughter in Paris and continue to enjoy critical accolade with impunity," she'd said. It had seemed normal when it left her mouth but then she'd seen the look on the face of her friend who was at her side.

She'd appointed that friend to keep an eye on her at these events. To make sure she never accepted his offers to share a cab, to instead slip her arm through hers and steer her toward the subway so that the worst that happened was a little twinge of regret that would pass along with her frozen margarita haze. The only thing about him that was indelible was the image he made standing in traffic in the blazing pink and orange of the city-street sunset, one hand stretched out with a cigarette to hail a cab, a wisp of smoke drifting against the deeper gray of his custom-made three-piece suit, dark black hair and eyes luminous. She'd spend half a block looking back at him while she chatted about other things with her friend. But the friend had since moved.

The sex club had been a thing they'd all been talking about over drinks that night. A week earlier she'd been searching for a spot where they could have the happy hour when she'd come across a Yelp review. Though it was under nightlife, it didn't seem to be a bar. Three reviews in she realized it was a swingers club and so she quickly chose a spot, sent out an invite, and then spent the rest of the afternoon consumed by how many stars swingers gave for things like clean towels.

It was good for conversation that evening when a quiet moment reminded them all that work friends are not friend friends. They looked up the reviews on their phones and read out loud the most amusing ones. He was sitting next to her and showed her the site for the place. The pricing list showed that Wednesday was the cheapest night of the week and things got progressively more expensive from there.

"It says if you're a guy, you need to have a woman with you to get in," he said. She gestured to the ignored line of women standing behind all the men at the bar who were fixated on televised sports. "You've got your pick."

"What about you? Would you go?"

In the bright lights of the bar with relative sobriety and the practiced steadiness that comes from being around people you know professionally, she wasn't so much in his sway. But even removed from his proposition, visiting the club intrigued her.

"I'm curious about it. But I don't want to be pawed at by creepy men."

"We'd go together. We wouldn't do anything with anyone. We could have a safe word if things get uncomfortable."

"What would our safe word be?"

"Mattress."

"I don't think mattress is the safest safe word in a sex club."

"Let's just go see what it's like."

She didn't answer in any way really. They resumed conversation with everyone else but soon talk strayed, as did their friends, and there they still were.

"Should we go?" was all he said and they set off.

Now here they were in the lobby, money already exchanged. The hostess saw their uneasiness and put down her phone.

"I promise you, you won't regret it in the morning," she reassured them. She opened a ledger. "What's your name?" she asked him.

"Asa Phillips." That was not his name.

"And yours?"

How did she not have a fake name for these situations? Why did he have such a readily available fake name for these situations?

"She's Liza."

"I'm Liza."

They walked inside to what looked surprisingly identical to a VFW hall. An empty VFW hall. Small faux-wood tables with cheap metal and leatherette chairs dotted the room. Along one wall were covered chafing dishes with sternos and a folding table that held tremendous Costco tubs of pretzels and Nilla wafers, as well as pitchers of water and juice and dinky plastic cups. The TV screen above the buffet table showed sports, while on the one across from the entrance a POV blow job was in progress.

Tucked in the corner was a bar that had no alcohol on display. A man in a burgundy vest stood behind it, tending to nothing, his eyes as mysteriously empty as the shelves behind him. "Can we get alcohol? Is this a real bar?" they asked. "We cannot serve alcohol," he

said. "But I can get you whatever you like." This con-
founded them and so they were quiet.

"Would you like a tour?" the barless bartender asked
with no inflection in tone. "Yes," they both said in
relief. This was ideal. They'd see everything there
was to see, maybe have a drink of – juice? – after, and
then leave. A story but not one so sordid that they
couldn't tell it at a party.

The bartender left his post and walked them down a
hallway with three doors on either side. He opened
each as he went. They peeked in but there was nothing to see except dingy flat mattresses that filled the
entire floor space in all but two of them. "These are
private rooms. You can go in there and shut the door
for privacy or leave it open if you want people to
watch or join you." "Oh," they said and nodded ap-
preciatively, trying to match his detachment as though
he were telling them how many miles per gallon a car
they were considering buying got. They reached a
large plate-glass window that gave a view of a room
with a soft pink glow and a pillowy floor that shone
with cheap satin. Next to it was a smaller version of
the same. "These are the orgy rooms," he said. "If you
go in, you can wear only underwear or a towel with
nothing on underneath." For orgies, the rooms were
distinctly lacking in participants.

"Where are the people?" he whispered to her. With no one around, the bartender could hear him though he gave no sign.

"I don't know," she whispered back.

"Um, so where is everybody?" he asked the bartender.

"We don't open till 9," he said.

How was it not even 9 yet? It felt like the middle of the night.

"Oh, I hate to be the first one at the orgy," he said but the bartender just turned and led them to the locker rooms. It was as humid as if hundreds of people had already been having sex in there all day. "This is where you can change. There are towels if you need." And the tour was over.

"We're just going to have a seat out there for a minute," he told the bartender and they all walked back down the hallway together silently. They both sat at a table in front of the Nilla wafers and the bartender stacked and unstacked plastic cups.

"What do you want to do?" he asked her.

"Well there's no one here. How much longer are we going to wait for people to show up? We already did the tour."

"I mean, do you want to go into one of those private rooms?" He paused. "With me?"

It seemed absurd but this she had not thought about. She'd been so focused on not doing anything with anybody when they got there that she never considered that something would happen between the two of them.

Just then his phone rang. It didn't just ring, it flashed multicolor lights around the room. He held it up. "Mom," it said in tall white letters. It seemed to mean every mom everywhere and she thought of her own and then tried not to.

"Does she have an alarm on you? Does she know you're in a sex club?"

"I have to take this. I'll be back," he said and walked off.

"Don't leave me alone…" she called out to him but he was gone. "In a sex club," she said to herself. She focused on the sports screen but that seemed too pointedly to be ignoring the situation, so instead she watched the blow job. The girl was so blonde and so eyelinered and had such round enormous breasts and the penis that projected from the bottom of the screen was so smooth and slender and pink that it was almost anime.

She hadn't noticed that he'd sat back down next to her. "So…" he said.

"I'm not sure." She hesitated. She thought of the rooms that were mattressed to the door, where there was literally no room for debate. "I definitely don't want to go into one of the ones where there's not even room to stand."

It would be like when she learned to drive."Turn right here," the instructor said and she did. And there she was on the Jackie Robinson Parkway, the twistiest, deadliest way to vehicularly travel from Queens to Brooklyn. She had hugged the car as close as possible to the high stone walls and prayed for a rapidly approaching exit.

"But I don't want to be out here anymore," she said.

"OK," he said to her, and to the bartender, "Uh, we'll take a room."

The bartender put down the cups and picked up a ring of keys and they followed him. She pointed out one of the rooms that had some allowance for standing.

"Don't take long," the bartender said, looking at her.

"What does that even mean?" she said and then closed the door in his face and locked it.

One bare red bulb illuminated the room and whatever switch controlled it, there was no accommodation for it to be turned off in there. Is red light flattering? She looked around and then finally up to check. You would think a sex club would have a mirror but no.

The smell of air freshener was overpowering, a scent that was olfactory-gland-numbingly sweet with no distinguishing notes. She knew she'd smelled it in all sorts of places before but never had it defined an experience like this. "This smells just like a sex club," is a phrase she knew she'd have to stop herself from saying for the rest of her life.

They leaned against the wall facing each other. Between them was a vaguely African painting that looked like sand art from the 70s but they hadn't even wasted money on using sand to make it. A faceless couple touched feet.

"What's this?" he said.

"Foot sex?"

He kissed her and they awkwardly made out for a minute. He stepped back.

"What we do is up to you. I don't want to pressure you into anything."

In considering their surroundings, she was disgusted by what she saw but terrified of what she didn't. Bodily fluids that would light up the room in blacklight and bedbugs and crabs and microorganisms whose names she did not even know probably. But she loved an experience and that bug was bigger than the others.

"Do you have condoms?"

"I do not," he said slowly as he realized he had not considered this on their walk over. "They must have condoms here, right?"

"Jesus. What brand are they going to have?" she said. "Probably some ineffective generic one that already comes with diseases pre-loaded."

"Let me go see."

A minute later he returned with a comical armload of bubblegum-pink-packaged condoms and a bewildered look.

"Did you ask for this many?"

"No, I just asked the guy for condoms and this is what he gave me." He threw them in a heap on the bed. She inspected a wrapper.

"I guess this is OK."

Her attention was still on the farcical pile of condoms when she felt his hands steadily maneuver her against the wall. He pressed into her. "I'm going to seduce you now," he said and she laughed at the absurdity of saying such a thing so that her mouth was wide open and their teeth clicked when he went in to kiss her. But he was serious and his lips steadied hers and she was soon overcome. Where he had been tentative before he was now deliberate. His hands and mouth and tongue were well-calibrated as they traveled her face, her mouth, her neck, and her chest. She loosened her dress.

He sat down on the edge of the mattress and carefully removed all but the pants of his expensive suit, his starched white shirt, his heavy silk tie, his gold cuff links, and the tie clip etched with his initials and carefully laid them out. She'd often thought of him as an entire Wes Anderson movie in a single person. And so he struck her again, surrounded by his very particular accoutrements in that cinematic oversaturated red room.

"I'm not looking for human affection," he said as he finished placing everything down.

That he had to qualify it as human struck her as strange. She pictured that rhesus monkey experiment where they took the baby away from its mother and gave it a horrifying-looking plastic-head and terry-cloth-body substitute. You could see on the frightened monkey's face that it knew but it had no choice for survival other than to cling to the wire shell.

"OK," she said as he stood up and kissed her throat, wrapped his arms around her and lowered her to the bed.

"I'm not looking for a girlfriend. I'm really happy with my life the way it is." It sounded like a conversation he'd had with himself before.

"We're in a sex club," she said. "So I didn't think you were looking for a girlfriend."

She could feel the sheets leaving tiny scratch marks against her skin.

"These sheets are all I can think about."

"They're a worry," he said.

"Maybe they were just cleaned because we're the first ones here." The false hope in her voice was for herself.

"Today," he said. "Do you want me to put my jacket down?"

"No, it's Brooks Brothers. Forget it."

He covered her with feathery kisses and then moved his tongue so deftly and gently that thoughts of the sheets were extinguished. "Your skin is so soft," he said. He traced his way back up to her mouth. He tasted sour and bitter, of her and tobacco, and as he slowly dry humped her, the curve of him became more apparent as it strained against his pants.

"Do you want to take them off?" he said.

She did. Underneath his navy-and-white patterned boxers were of such good quality that they transcended what you would think was possible of cotton. He removed them less carefully than he had everything else. She slid her lips over him and he arched back and gently brushed her face and hair with a startling tenderness. She sat up and kissed him.

"This mattress," she said.

"So gross," he said.

But they really had no choice but to move fully onto it. There were some pillows that had never seen sleep and she picked them up by just the very ends and tossed them off the bed, along with a wedge that she tried to barely touch. It was then that she realized she only had one shoe on.

"I lost my shoe. I hate to think of where it is."

"You've got your shoes on?"

"I'm not risking my feet touching the ground in here."

"Good point."

At the bar her shoe had also fallen off while her feet were dangling from a bar stool. He had retrieved it from the floor and tried to slip it on her foot but she swooped her hand down to take it from him and put it back on herself, unwilling to be some cliche.

"Forget the shoe, I'll find it later," she said now.

It was more to herself than to him because he was lost in kissing her, breaking it up with small licks and deep bites to her neck. She had the disconcerting thought that she'd been in entire relationships with men who had never displayed such ardor in similar moments. "You smell good," he said.

"You, too. Like cigarettes. But I like it."

"And cologne," he said, though she couldn't smell it.

He stopped suddenly. "What was that?" He lifted his head for a noise she could not detect. All she heard was his heart as it pounded against her chest.

"What is it?"

"I heard someone."

"So? What do you think is going to happen? That you're going to get busted for having sex in a sex club?" She laughed and he waved his hands in front of her face, part in jest, but partly from real panic.

"What are you afraid of?"

"They'll send me back to Guantanamo Bay."

If he had tried to quiet her laugh before, it was impossible now. Fear another Holocaust or find it hilarious. Get mad that you could get thrown off a plane or fly in the face of it. She saw in his face that he was making one of those decisions. The alarm left his expression. He pressed his lips to her and his voice was thick as he said into her ear, "Fuck it, we paid our money." Of all the thoughts she'd had about why he took such care with his appearance and spent money with such profligacy, this one had never occurred to her.

The temperature between them had gone up a good 20 degrees and as he came she could smell his cologne in a warm wave. It was bespoke but the perfumer had cleverly hidden within it the provoking memory of high-school boys and department-store Polo.

She let go and gave in and when her eyelids flicked open she saw him sitting astride her with his beautiful mussed-up hair and a sweet and goofy smile on his face. There was something like enlightenment. She searched her mind for things that she knew would be painful, those behind her and things that she had not yet faced. She knew this relief from her always anxious mind would pass quickly and so she took one moment and kept it still and to remember tied it to that image of him.

She took a breath and then set about to find her lost shoe and her clothing and all the things she owned that she would run under scalding water and harsh soap, whether that was advisable for the fabric or not.

He struggled with his stiff Italian leather shoes that he had once told her were polished daily at his desk by a person who came around to his law office.

"I didn't expect this to be my Thursday night," he said.

"Me neither."

"I would do this again. I don't mean here."

"Me, too."

She found her sweater and as she put it on, he came up behind her and nuzzled her neck.

"I wish we could leave here without going back out there," she said. "There must be people by now."

He gestured upward. "Oh. These walls don't go all the way to the ceiling." He was right. They were false furniture showroom walls.

"Everybody heard us," she said.

"Us and our hypochondriac routine about how gross this place is."

"You go out first. I'll walk behind you. Don't stop for anything until we're outside."

He opened the door and she tried to fix her gaze on his back but she saw an elderly nearly skeletal couple sitting on a bench facing the room they'd been in. Their dead eyes and stilted movements made them unreal, like a set from an amusement-park horror tunnel, until the man made eye contact with her as he fondled his companion's bare breast. She ducked her eyes down until they were in fresh air.

They didn't speak until they were several buildings away.

"Well," he finally said.

"Well."

"I'm going to go get some cigarettes. Want to come?"

"Sure. Then I'm going to get a cab."

"OK."

He seemed to want to unburden himself of something. After half a block he said, "My dad had a heart attack the other week. That's why I had to take that call."

"I know something about things like that," she said.

They stepped into a 7-Eleven. The cashier smiled at them, which was an uncharacteristic move for a 7-Eleven cashier, and she felt like he could tell. Really she felt like everyone could.

"Parliament Lights," he said to the cashier.

"Do you want anything?" he asked her.

"No, I'm fine."

He looked around as he was rung up. There was a hand-cream display next to the register. "What about Nivea? Do you want some Nivea?"

"I'm good."

On the sidewalk he lit up and then hailed a cab for her.

"I think that cashier knew," she said.

"He probably goes to my mosque."

A taxi stopped, and he opened the door and kissed her on the cheek. As she stepped inside the car, she heard him call out to her as he walked away.

"Where we were is under NDA," he shouted. "But if you write about it, start at the red door."

Acknowledgments

A collection is built story by story and this one wouldn't have been possible without the encouragement I got from all of those who published these stories first: Ample Remains ("Take a Number"), *superfroot* ("Not My Baby"), *Meat for Tea: The Valley Review* ("Sic Transit Memoria"), *Storm Cellar* ("Lives of the Saints"), Wigleaf ("The Copy Artist"), No Contact ("Bill of Goods"), Litro Magazine ("Out of the Blue"), and Vol. 1 Brooklyn ("Pushed" and "Thursday Night Special").